A SPECIAL OCCASION

Written by Pauline Cartwright
Illustrated by Philip Webb

Mr Acker had lots of hats.
He had a hat that he wore
when he went fishing.
There were flies all around the band.
"I do so well when I wear this hat,"
Mr Acker said.

4

Mr Acker had a hat that he wore
when he was in the garden.
It had a wide brim to keep the sun off,
and a string to keep his hat on if the wind blew.
"I feel so comfortable in this hat,"
he said.

Mr Acker had a hat that he wore
when he went out.
It was a smart felt one
with a tiny, tiny feather in the band.
"I look so important in this hat,"
he said.

Mr Acker had a hat that he wore
when he went for a walk.
It was a checked cap
with a button on top and a peak at the front.
"I like saying 'hello' when I wear this hat,"
he said.

10

11

Mr Acker had a hat that he wore
when he went to the beach.
It was a floppy sunhat
and it was red to match his bathing-suit.
"I have such a good time when I wear this hat,"
he said.

13

He had lots of other hats.
He kept them in case of a Special Occasion.

One day a sign went up in the town.
MARDI GRAS on SATURDAY
Everyone wear a
BIG, BRIGHT
FANTASTIC
hat!

Mr Acker hurried home
and looked in his cupboard.
He had a big hat
but it wasn't bright and fantastic.

He had a bright hat
but it wasn't fantastic and big.

He had a fantastic hat
but it wasn't big and bright.
A Special Occasion
and he didn't have a hat to wear!

For a while, Mr Acker felt very sad.
Then he said to himself,
"There's no use moping.
I'll just have to make one."
So he did.

Mr Acker made a VERY fantastic hat.
It was very big and very bright.
He made it from sugar and butter
and eggs and flour and cocoa.
Mr Acker made an ENORMOUS chocolate-cake hat!

He decorated it
with silver balls
and with sugar flowers
and with long twirling ribbons.
Right on the top,
he fixed a big green candle.

On Saturday, he put on his big bright fantastic hat—
his chocolate-cake hat with the candle on top.
Off he went to the Mardi Gras.
Everyone was wearing a hat.
The bands played all day,
and the people danced and danced
wearing their big bright fantastic hats.

At night, when the sky grew dim,
the people couldn't see to dance.
Then, Mr Acker lit the big green candle
on the top of his big bright fantastic hat.
All the people followed Mr Acker,
dancing until they were too tired
and too hungry to dance any more.

Then Mr Acker took off his hat.
He gave the silver balls
and the sugar flowers to the children.
He cut up the enormous chocolate-cake hat
and every dancer at the Mardi Gras had an enormous piece!
Round his neck Mr Acker hung the long twirling ribbons.
He would take them home so he could always remember
the very special occasion.